In the Eye of the Hurricane

by

Eduardo Machado

SAMUEL FRENCH

FOUNDED 1830

NEW YORK HOLLYWOOD LONDON TORONTO

SAMUELFRENCH.COM

ISBN 978-0-573-66043-6   Printed in U.S.A.   #7140

IMPORTANT BILLING AND CREDIT REQUIREMENTS

IN THE EYE OF THE HURRICANE premiered at the Actors Theatre of Louisville Humana Festival of New American Plays on March 14, 1991. The production was directed by Anne Bogart, with scenic design by Paul Owen, lighting design by Karl Haas, sound design by Darron West, costume design by Michael Krass, and casting by Jay Binder. The stage manager was Craig Weindling, assistant stage manager Henry Meiman, with dramaturgy by Michael Bigelow Dixon. The cast was as follows:

MANUELA	Diane D'Aquila
MARIA	Lynn Cohen
MARIO	Christopher McCann
OSCAR	Bob Burrus
SONIA	Pamela Stewart
HUGO	Rafael Baez
ROSA	Suzanne Costallos
ANTONIO	Robert Machray
FULGENCIO	V Craig Heidenreich
MILICIANO	Michael Weis
MILICIANO	Arthur Aulisi

CHARACTERS

MANUELA, *lady of the house*
MARIA JOSEFA, *her mother*
MARIO, *her brother*
OSCAR, *her husband*
SONIA, *her daughter*
HUGO, *her orphaned nephew*
ROSA, *her maid*
ANTONIO, *her cousin*
FULGENCIO, *a bus driver*
MILICIANO 1
MILICIANO 2

TIME

Act One: a spring day, 1960.
Act Two: the following day.

PLACE

Guanabacoa, Cuba

For Hariette,
December 1989.

ACT ONE

Scene 1

(A dining room. A large mahogany table, modern in style, many chairs around it. Ledgers stacked on the table. A sideboard. Doors leading to a tropical garden. Beyond it, the field where the buses are kept. Next to the field, the garage. Yet all we see on stage is the furniture and doors upstage center.)

*(****MARIO**** runs in, ****MARIA JOSEFA**** follows him.)*

MARIA JOSEFA. Let me read it.

MARIO. No!

MARIA JOSEFA. Come on, read it to your mother. I'm your mother.

MARIO. I'll tear it up before I let you read it!

MARIA JOSEFA. You shouldn't keep secrets from your mother.

MARIO. I'm forty-five years old.

MARIA JOSEFA. Come on, son. You're fifty. Don't lie about your age to your mother. You're fifty!

MARIO. I was born in 1908.

MARIA JOSEFA. One nine zero eight from 1960 is fifty-two. You're fifty-two.

MARIO. Mama!

MARIA JOSEFA. Believe me, I remember when I gave birth to you. I have a daughter who's already in her sixties; she lies about her age also.

MARIO. All right, I'm fifty-two, more reason that you should give me a little bit of privacy and not try to read my mail.

MARIA JOSEFA. Which tart wrote you this one?

MARIO. None of your business.

MARIA JOSEFA. The last one…

MARIO. Shut up!

MARIA JOSEFA. Never married, that's the tragedy of your life.

(**ROSA** *enters.*)

ROSA. Here it is, the treat.

MARIA JOSEFA. Now that's a good girl.

(**MARIO** *exits.*)

Where are you going? Never answers me –

(**ROSA** *hands her a glass of lemonade.* **MARIA JOSEFA** *drinks.*)

Yum, lemonade, bitter and sweet.

ROSA. I just like the sweet part.

MARIA JOSEFA. That's why you're the maid and I'm the employer.

ROSA. *(Hurt)* Maria Josefa?!

MARIA JOSEFA. Don't be hurt. It's a fact, the only way to be successful in life is to enjoy the… *(She falls asleep)*

ROSA. What?

MARIA JOSEFA. *(Coming back)* …bittersweet.

ROSA. Success.

MARIA JOSEFA. Lemonade.

ROSA. Fidel Castro, he's the most successful man in Cuba.

MARIA JOSEFA. For now.

ROSA. Your daughter likes him, she thinks he's a hero.

MARIA JOSEFA. Just because she thinks it doesn't mean I agree.

ROSA. It's hard working here. I don't know who to be loyal to.

MARIA JOSEFA. Be loyal to me, you're in my will.

ROSA. One feels safe when you have one person who's the boss. I thought Mr. Hernandez was it – that would have been easy – but Mario, he's so –

MARIA JOSEFA. Careful! Remember he's my son. He's my son.

ROSA. I like him. I'm used to him. The cleaning lady doesn't like him. He's always ordering her around.

MARIA JOSEFA. With Mario, ordering is a need, not an obligation.

ROSA. And you and your daughter are always in conflict about dinner plans.

MARIA JOSEFA. Listen to what I tell you and you'll be fine.

ROSA. I've been working here now for ten years, I think I've figured out a way to survive – one just has to get by.

MARIA JOSEFA. "Getting by" is not enough, my dear. You have to be greedy. Sit down, relax and listen to me.

(**MANUELA** *enters.*)

MANUELA. Rosa, the tomato sauce is burning.

ROSA. Oh no! Oh, my God! I'm so sorry. I got carried away talking.

MARIA JOSEFA. Talking to me, I'll go see if I can save it. *(She exits)*

MANUELA. Mama, let Rosa.

ROSA. I'm so sorry.

MANUELA. Go and help her. She's not strong enough to be cooking. What's this? Lemonade. With sugar. I told you to be strict about –

ROSA. It's hard. She doesn't know how sick –

MANUELA. But you know how sick she is. I've explained it to you.

ROSA. But I feel sorry for your mother. She –

MANUELA. Don't manipulate me.

ROSA. But she manipulates me.

MANUELA. Don't let her.

ROSA. Not so easy, I have a kind heart.

MANUELA. I have to finish last night's accounts. Try to get her to take some medicine.

ROSA. Fine.

MANUELA. Take her out to the patio.

ROSA. Fine.

MANUELA. Don't burn anything else.

ROSA. Fine.

> (**ROSA** *exits.* **MANUELA** *sits down and goes through the ledgers.*)

MANUELA. *(To herself, sighs)* I feel safe here in my dining room. It is my domain.

> (**MARIA JOSEFA** *enters.*)

MARIA JOSEFA. What, dear?

MANUELA. I was just…

MARIA JOSEFA. Just what?

MANUELA. Talking to myself.

MARIA JOSEFA. Talking to yourself? That's a bad sign, dear. That's the beginning of a deteriorating mind, and a deteriorated mind leads to a collapsing body… *(She wonders off.)*

MANUELA. Mama, what? Finish what you are saying.

> *(Pause.)*

MARIA JOSEFA. My father talked to himself. So did my husband and look what happened to them.

MANUELA. What happened to them, what?

MARIA JOSEFA. They died.

MANUELA. Not of natural causes. Neither one of them died of natural causes, Mama.

MARIA JOSEFA. What's the difference.

MANUELA. Their deaths were violent. Fate. Accidental.

MARIA JOSEFA. Accidents? May God forgive them for their accidents.

MANUELA. Then Mama, how could it have anything to do with their minds deteriorating, 'cause they talked to themselves? When they didn't have deaths caused by sickness. They didn't have normal deaths.

MARIA JOSEFA. So?

MANUELA. Their deaths had nothing to do with their mental or physical condition.

MARIA JOSEFA. Maybe.

MANUELA. Sometimes a person has a thought, and in order for that thought, idea, to become real, you have to say it aloud.

MARIA JOSEFA. So what was this great thought?

MANUELA. Never mind.

MARIA JOSEFA. I want to hear it, Mama wants to hear it.

MANUELA. I said, "I feel safe here in my dining room. It is my domain."

MARIA JOSEFA. See, I'm right. You're in trouble. One foot in the grave. Feeling safe. How can a woman feel safe?

MANUELA. You're so pessimistic, Mama.

(She puts some of the ledgers inside the sideboard and locks it)

MARIA JOSEFA. Feeling safe means that you are tempting fate, playing with disaster. Dangerous to feel safe, Manuela. It leads you right into violence and death.

MANUELA. Safety?!

MARIA JOSEFA. Yes.

MANUELA. Mama!

MARIA JOSEFA. Believe me.

MANUELA. Oh, Mama. Please… *(She lights a cigarette)*

MARIA JOSEFA. Give me one.

*(**MANUELA** gives her a cigarette.)*

A puff from a cigarette. Now that's a sensation.

MANUELA. If I can't feel safe in my own dining room, then where?

MARIA JOSEFA. The only thing that makes me feel safe is counting money. Counting, adding, seeing the result. Profit, safety. Let me count.

MANUELA. I already counted last night's take. Too bad for you.

MARIA JOSEFA. Did you make the deposit yourself?

MANUELA. Yes.

MARIA JOSEFA. Good.

MANUELA. Oh, God!

MARIA JOSEFA. What?

MANUELA. I got a cramp in my calf.

MARIA JOSEFA. I don't feel sorry for you.

MANUELA. God does it hurt.

MARIA JOSEFA. No sympathy from me.

MANUELA. Who's asking you for sympathy?

MARIA JOSEFA. It's because of that exercise bike you bought yourself. A bicycle that goes nowhere, you just sit and pedal, like a moron. Who ever heard of a woman in her sixties exercising?

MANUELA. Gringos.

MARIA JOSEFA. I never thought you'd grow up to be so vain.

MANUELA. Smart, not vain. It's beginning to go away.

MARIA JOSEFA. Going to the sauna was bad enough, then dyeing your hair.

MANUELA. I like Oscar to keep interested in me.

MARIA JOSEFA. If you want to keep your husband interested, learn how to be a better cook.

MANUELA. The maids cook well enough…

MARIA JOSEFA. Give a man a special kind of seasoning when you cook. The right spices that make up your own special flavor. That's what men want from their wives. 'Specially by the time they are sixty.

MANUELA. Fifty-nine.

MARIA JOSEFA. What a vain girl you grew up to be. That taste that he can only get at home, that's what you should –

MANUELA. You've managed to depress me, and I was feeling so…

MARIA JOSEFA. Sure?

MANUELA. Rub my leg.

MARIA JOSEFA. It's a curse to get old.

MANUELA. I'm not old yet, not inside, still look all right outside.

MARIA JOSEFA. That's because you haven't had any disappointment.

MANUELA. I'm disappointed that you refuse to rub my leg.

MARIA JOSEFA. I want another cigarette.

(**MANUELA** *lights her another and one for herself.*)

True disappointment with life, that's the curse that brings old age. You've never been disappointed so you think you're young.

MANUELA. Maybe I'll never know disappointment. Maybe I'll stay young forever. Things now are –

MARIA JOSEFA. Going to get better?

MANUELA. Yes.

MARIA JOSEFA. I've never trusted men with beards.

MANUELA. It's only a trademark.

MARIA JOSEFA. They look like they don't bathe.

MANUELA. He'll be more honest than –

MARIA JOSEFA. Don't you dare say a word against Batista!

MANUELA. Never mind.

(**MARIA JOSEFA** *looks out the doors.* **MANUELA** *looks over the accounts.*)

MARIA JOSEFA. One of the lilies of the valley has come out to look at me.

MANUELA. It's too early in the year for lilies to bloom. They're still little plants. In a month –

MARIA JOSEFA. No, look over there. (*She points out the door*) You see it now, sweetheart.

MANUELA. It's early, it's an early riser, that one.

MARIA JOSEFA. Flowers don't know about time.

MANUELA. Well, maybe not time, but cycles, seasons.

MARIA JOSEFA. No, I don't think so. I think they just are.

Once a whole field of lilies of the valley bloomed for me. You don't believe me? But they did! It's when we lived in a much more rural part of town, Guanabacoa was much more rural then, than now. More open fields, and we lived next to a huge field. It was the night before my first communion, I had been fasting all day, so I could be clean when the sacred sacrament entered my body.

(**MARIA JOSEFA** *lights a cigarette. Pause.*)

MANUELA. And?

MARIA JOSEFA. What… ?

MANUELA. Did you fall asleep?

MARIA JOSEFA. The day before my first communion?

MANUELA. No, just now.

MARIA JOSEFA. And it bloomed, a field full of lilies, and I knew the holy sacrament wanted me. (*She laughs*) Wanted me, that was the last moment I ever had in my life that was simple. And today "he" only shows me one.

MANUELA. Maybe it's not just for you.

MARIA JOSEFA. I know I'm dying.

MANUELA. What are you talking about, Mama?

MARIA JOSEFA. I asked him to let me know, how long, how much more.

MANUELA. You should rest before lunch.

MARIA JOSEFA. Take me to my room.

MANUELA. Yes.

MARIA JOSEFA. Read me last night's figures.

MANUELA. Yes. (*She takes the ledgers*)

MARIA JOSEFA. Make a profit?

MANUELA. Of course.

MARIA JOSEFA. Busier than usual?

MANUELA. Yes. Rosa!

ROSA. (*Entering*) Yes?

MANUELA. Bring me Mama's medicine.

*(***MANUELA*** *and* **MARIA JOSEFA** *exit.)*

ROSA. When will I get a moment's rest.

*(***ROSA*** *sits and closes her eyes.* **MARIO** *enters; he has a packet watch, he looks at the time and then begins to flip it in his hand.)*

MARIO. On break?

ROSA. You timing me?

MARIO. With this...See, gold, heavy, feel it.

ROSA. Leave me alone.

MARIO. Solid, heavy, strong like me.

ROSA. Dense. Like your mind. Always ticking away.

MARIO. Dense, no. Intricate, full of levers to keep it running.

ROSA. Evil.

MARIO. I've never taken advantage of you, never once pinched your butt.

ROSA. You never once looked at my tits.

MARIO. So what?

ROSA. There's something wrong with a man that doesn't look at my tits.

MARIO. Maybe I have manners, taste.

ROSA. Never knew a man who didn't notice my –

MARIO. Breast! Don't say "tits," "breast."

ROSA. You're the only man who's never looked at them.

MARIO. Show them to me now.

ROSA. No!

MARIO. Now's your chance.

ROSA. Your mother's medicine, I have to take it to her.

MARIO. Let me admire them.

ROSA. Evil.

MARIO. Let me see, show me.

ROSA. You're supposed to sneak a look, I'm not supposed to exhibit them in front of you. One little look when I'm not looking. *(She exits)*

MARIO. Sneak a look? I'm supposed to enjoy seeing your blubbery boobs by sneaking a look? Nationalize? Bullshit! Nationalize. Fuck you, God!

*(****HUGO**** enters.)*

HUGO. Were you calling me?

MARIO. No.

HUGO. I heard you yelling out.

MARIO. I was cursing God, not calling you.

HUGO. Sorry.

*(****MARIO**** grabs ****HUGO****'s arm.)*

MARIO. Fight me.

HUGO. I don't feel like it.

MARIO. Come on, show me your strength.

HUGO. All right.

*(They start to arm-wrestle. ****MARIO**** twists ****HUGO****'s arm.)*

MARIO. See?

HUGO. All right! Please stop! You won! You win!

MARIO. That's right, I won.

HUGO. You're stronger than me, so what?

MARIO. You better get strong.

HUGO. I will. *(He exits)*

MARIO. Some things, I win. I'm going to outlive you, Maria Josefa.

*(He begins to weep. ****MANUELA**** enters.)*

MANUELA. You're crying, Mario.

MARIO. Leave me alone.

MANUELA. What is it?

MARIO. I got a cold.

MANUELA. How did you get it?

MARIO. I don't know, how does one get anything…

MANUELA. By working for it.

*(****MARIO**** laughs.)*

MARIO. Really, is that how?

MANUELA. Don't be sarcastic.

MARIO. You seem to know so much, sister.

MANUELA. What are you implying?

MARIO. Nothing, I'm stuffed up, out of…

MANUELA. Out of what?

MARIO. Place, out of place.

MANUELA. Well –

MARIO. It's Mama.

MANUELA. Yes.

MARIO. Her illness. What's it called again?

MANUELA. Diabetes.

MARIO. Have you told her yet?

MANUELA. I'm not going to tell her.

MARIO. That sugar, all that sweet sugar water is killing her. The syrup she has for blood has gone out of control. *(He starts to cry)*

MANUELA. Everyone thinks that their mother will never die. I don't like seeing you sad.

MARIO. I'm crying from anger!

MANUELA. Never mind, Mario.

MARIO. Mother's illness has made me angry at you and your husband.

MANUELA. You're my brother and I've tried –

MARIO. Angry at you.

MANUELA. Tried to reach you, but –

MARIO. Your husband –

MANUELA. Stop your accusations.

MARIO. I haven't accused anybody.

MANUELA. We would have been nowhere, if Oscar hadn't come into my life. He saved all of us.

MARIO. All but Papa.

MANUELA. Please. It's not my fault that Mama has…It's not my fault that Papa…

MARIO. Right, let's not bring it up.

MANUELA. Fine.

MARIO. Fine.

(*They embrace.*)

MANUELA. Lunch will be ready soon.

(**MARIO** *looks out the window.*)

MARIO. Here he comes.

MANUELA. Who?

MARIO. Your husband.

MANUELA. Look, see him. He has a bunch of gladioluses for Mama. Look at the way he's talking to Hugo. He reassures your nephew with a touch, how he takes care of your dead brother's son. How my husband has protected us, all of us. And you resent him?

MARIO. Right.

MANUELA. Go and say hello to Mama.

MARIO. I drove to the corner and bought her a carton of Lucky Strikes -

MANUELA. Here.

(*She goes into a drawer, and takes out a syringe*)

You inject her, she thinks you have a steadier hand.

MARIO. Where's the medicine?

MANUELA. Rosa has it.

MARIO. Lucky Strikes.

MANUELA. She'll like that. Steal me a pack.

MARIO. If she lets me. (*He exits*)

MANUELA. Hello, flowers for me?

OSCAR. (*Offstage*) No.

MANUELA. I know – for my mother.

(**OSCAR** *enters.*)

OSCAR. How can I?

MANUELA. How can you what?

OSCAR. Live without your mother.

MANUELA. We'll find a way.

OSCAR. I never had a mother.

MANUELA. Yes.

OSCAR. I thought that the only good thing about that was that I would never lose her, my mother.

MANUELA. And now you have to go through losing mine.

OSCAR. All of the pain and none of the ownership.

MANUELA. You're like a son to her.

OSCAR. But, not a son. "Like" is not the same thing as. "he is my son." Mario is her son. Like being in cahoots with the new regime, doesn't mean that "you are" the new order.

MANUELA. Give Fidel a chance.

OSCAR. It's getting tougher.

MANUELA. Got the cash?

OSCAR. Sonia's surprise?

MANUELA. Yes!

OSCAR. Right, we're getting her a car today, right…

MANUELA. How could you forget?!

OSCAR. I didn't forget. It's in my pocket and ready. You know me. I like to tease you 'cause you're so stubborn.

MANUELA. I love you.

(**HUGO** *enters.*)

OSCAR. Look. (*He shows her an envelope with bills in it*)

HUGO. What is that?

MANUELA. We're getting Sonia her car.

HUGO. Lucky Sonia.

OSCAR. Don't be jealous. Doesn't pay to be jealous.

HUGO. I'm not jealous.

MANUELA. Good.

HUGO. Is it going to be a brand-new one?

OSCAR. Yes, of course.

HUGO. And she'll be the first person to smell it, smell the leather on the seats. And push down on the clutch and change gears.

MANUELA. Maybe when you get older, she'll let you drive it.

HUGO. When she gets bored with it – she gets bored with everything because she gets so much.

MANUELA. So do you. When you're older...

HUGO. Fidel will make sure I have a car.

MANUELA. Not like the one we're going to buy Sonia, it's English.

HUGO. You already picked it out for her.

OSCAR. I did. It's a beauty.

HUGO. Fidel wants everyone to have everything equally.

MANUELA. You believe that?

HUGO. Well, he does...

(**MARIO** *enters.*)

MARIO. Fidel wants everyone to lose everything equally.

OSCAR. We're your family, Hugo. Only family give each other things.

MANUELA. That's right. Listen to my husband.

HUGO. Everything for the family.

MANUELA. Everything for, from, and in the family.

OSCAR. That's right. It's the only thing you can rely on, the only thing you can believe in.

HUGO. All right, how long do I have to wait for a car?

MANUELA. When Uncle decides that you've earned it.

HUGO. Uncle Oscar?

MARIO. Uncle Mario.

HUGO. Then I'll never see a car.

MARIO. You'll be driving a bus soon, like the rest of the family, so don't worry about cars.

MANUELA. No, he's going to school and become a foot specialist.

MARIO. A good profession for you.

HUGO. I'm going to talk to Grandma. Call when it's time for lunch.

MANUELA. Here, take her the gladioluses.

(**HUGO** *exits.*)

You tease him too much.

MARIO. I want him to be ready for it when it all falls apart.

MANUELA. What falls apart?

OSCAR. Get me some cafe. I need some cafe.

MANUELA. All right. I'll get Rosa to make it.

OSCAR. You make it better.

MANUELA. Not really.

OSCAR. For me you do.

MANUELA. All right. I've spoilt you.

OSCAR. I love it.

(**MANUELA** *exits.*)

MARIO. You got up early today.

OSCAR. Had a lot of errands.

MARIO. Couldn't wait to have cafe with me, I guess…

OSCAR. Had a lot on my mind.

MARIO. Of course, so did I.

OSCAR. In the afternoon, we'll go to Havana, and have a couple of drinks. ..

MARIO. Maybe I needed to talk to you this morning. We got problems!

OSCAR. Is it the number five? Is it burning oil again? We're gonna have to rebuild the motor on that one…

MARIO. We bought it used, we should have bought a new one.

OSCAR. It was a bargain. Besides, you gotta trust a bus that drove on the streets of Chicago, Illinois, USA.

MARIO. It's running fine. It's a different dilemma we're facing...It's hard to…

OSCAR. Who do you want to fire now?

MARIO. Nobody! Don't you see what's happening? Fidel is a Communist!

OSCAR. Fidel's no Communist. Don't start with that record again! Fidel's our boy! He got rid of Batista and that's all that matters.

MARIO. He conned us.

OSCAR. Shut up!

MARIO. So you did know about it. And you were not going to tell me?

OSCAR. It's only gossip.

MARIO. No it's not. I got a note today from Gilberto Valladares, my friend, who works in the Bureau of Information, for Fidel, where they write his speeches...

OSCAR. I want you to understand something. I want you to listen to me and understand one thing. ...You know me well enough...

MARIO. Like a book. I know you like a book.

OSCAR. We are a couple of years away from being millionaires. From turning our beachfront property into a beautiful hotel. All my life I've wanted a beautiful hotel with a casino standing beside it. And a golf course adjoining it. And the Gulf of Mexico facing it, like a beautiful blue painting. All my life, I've wanted to have a million dollars in my pocket. And no little rebellious punk is gonna cheat me out of my dreams!

MARIO. He already has.

OSCAR. Gossip. Mario the little gossip from –

MARIO. Oscar, please, respect me.

OSCAR. Gossip from Guanabacoa.

MARIO. I have proof. And it spells out Communism.

OSCAR. No.

MARIO. Yes!

OSCAR. Trust me.

MARIO. Look at my eye. How it's been twitching, my upper lip, from nerves, I can't get it to stop.

OSCAR. What did Valladares send you?

MARIO. Feel my hands, cold, clammy, frightened.

OSCAR. Show me.

MARIO. Here it is.

(**OSCAR** *reads.*)

It's a copy of a summons we're going to receive...Are you panicked?

OSCAR. No, of course not. Did you tell your sister?

MARIO. No.

OSCAR. Good, we should protect her…

MARIO. From the truth?

OSCAR. Yes.

MARIO. Protecting is almost like lying, isn't it?

OSCAR. No, it's what men have to do.

MARIO. That's why I told you. I would never tell my sister.

OSCAR. She must never see that summons. Because it's not going to happen, they are not going to confiscate the buses. Have you told her about the note?

MARIO. I wanted to tell you first. We only have a few days to come up with some sort of plan to fight back…

(**MANUELA** *enters.*)

MANUELA. The cafe.

OSCAR. *(Taking a sip)* See. Delicious!

MANUELA. What were you two screaming about?

OSCAR. Usual stuff.

MARIO. Income.

MANUELA. I heard Mario scream that Fidel is a Communist. Rosa just heard on the radio that he's giving a speech tonight, to declare his intentions. I thought he declared his intentions when he was fighting Batista. Has he found new ones? If he's a Communist, you know what that means?

OSCAR. What?

MANUELA. They don't believe in Christ. They don't believe in private ownership. I mean what is Fidel up to? You heard Hugo, that's dangerous talk.

OSCAR. This is a little country. What would Russia want with such a little country?

MANUELA. What they all want – a tan.

OSCAR. No, Russians live covered in snow. They're afraid of the sun. Mario, let's go.

MARIO. When will lunch finally be ready?

MANUELA. An hour.

MARIO. I'm hungry, tell her to hurry it up.

MANUELA. I will.

MARIO. Nervousness makes me want to eat.

MANUELA. Why are you so nervous?

OSCAR. Life – simple life makes your brother nervous.

(*He exits*)

MANUELA. You would have been poor without him, you'd still be driving a bus.

MARIO. We might be poor again.

MANUELA. Never.

MARIO. You don't respect me, do you, sister?

MANUELA. I'm a woman who knows the only man that she can trust and respect is her husband.

MARIO. Here, don't say anything. I promised him, he told me not to show it to you, but you should know. I don't get nervous by simple life, I have a reason to be scared.

(**MARIO** *hands* **MANUELA** *the summons. She starts to read it. Blackout.*)

Scene 2

(Lights up. **OSCAR** *is looking at the mirror. The note is in his hand.)*

OSCAR. Has someone disfigured my face? Why does my face feel crooked?

*(***MANUELA*** *enters.)*

MANUELA. Is it true, the note...?

OSCAR. Mario's friends always exaggerate.

MANUELA. But is it true, Oscar?!

OSCAR. Yes, I think it's all true.

MANUELA. And you were trying to keep it from me.

OSCAR. Protect you.

MANUELA. I thought we were partners in this business, that I was an equal.

OSCAR. I thought that with your mother dying that you couldn't take any more...

MANUELA. I can take anything. I know how to fight.

OSCAR. I had forgotten that you're made out of steel.

MANUELA. And you like it.

OSCAR. I love it.

MANUELA. Who do we appeal to?

OSCAR. We don't know, he's going to announce it tonight. Then all the other bus companies together, we'll have a plan, a strike, a war. We'll win.

MANUELA. Do they want to buy them from us or what?

OSCAR. No, take, they want to take them.

MANUELA. Steal them.

OSCAR. They will be the nation's – nationalized.

MANUELA. Another word for stealing.

OSCAR. We'll still own them as part of the collective "we," as part of the national "we." That's his plan. But you know plans have a way of being interrupted.

MANUELA. You're so calm.

OSCAR. We'll find a solution, we have time.

MANUELA. Don't tell Mama.

OSCAR. I won't.

MANUELA. She doesn't have to know.

OSCAR. You look lovely today.

MANUELA. I had a facial.

OSCAR. Thank God for facials, then.

MANUELA. Tell me the plans? Do we try to protest, organize a way to overthrow him? God, why does everything in this country have to be so brutal?

*(**OSCAR** puts his hand up Manuela's dress.)*

Oscar, answer me that, what does this country have against a ballot box?

OSCAR. Manuela.

MANUELA. We have to overthrow somebody else again.

OSCAR. Hmmmm, lovely.

MANUELA. Silk.

(Oscar's hands are up Manuela's dress.)

Expensive.

OSCAR. Thrilling.

MANUELA. That we can afford it?

OSCAR. That you still wear it so well.

MANUELA. Somebody might come in.

OSCAR. No.

MANUELA. Love me, don't you?

OSCAR. I want to keep touching, forever.

*(**MANUELA** starts to laugh.)*

Still get excited, when I put my hand up your dress.

MANUELA. This is the first time you've ever done it.

OSCAR. No, before…

MANUELA. Never, not me. Must have been somebody else's dress you put your hands up, someone who could afford silk…

OSCAR. Never.

MANUELA. Really?

OSCAR. Yes…

MANUELA. Always been ready and available to you in our bed, you never had to sneak a touch with me, wealth allows a woman to stay younger…

OSCAR. Thank God.

MANUELA. My mother resents me, resents my appearance because she ended her sexual – her needs so early, she stopped being a woman at such an early age. Too soon…and she thinks, knows, I'm still enjoying too much. Because of her struggles, so she resents the massages, the facial creams…

(**OSCAR** *kisses her.*)

OSCAR. Us.

MANUELA. Yes, us. Let's take a siesta after lunch.

OSCAR. Let's forget.

MANUELA. Forget, no.

OSCAR. That it's daytime.

HUGO. *(Entering)* Uncle Oscar, Mario needs you with him.

OSCAR. Now?!

MANUELA. Go, lunch is almost ready.

(**OSCAR** *and* **HUGO** *exit. We hear a bus drive in.* **MANUELA** *stands and looks out the doors.* **ROSA** *enters, sets the table.*)

ROSA. Looking at the garden? Is someone in it that's not supposed to be?

MANUELA. No, looking at the buses, the number eight just came in for its gasoline stop. On time, it's running on time today.

ROSA. How can you see the number from so far away?

MANUELA. I can't. I recognize the sound of the motor.

ROSA. They all sound the same to me.

MANUELA. Not to me. It's all I have.

ROSA. The buses?

MANUELA. Yes, they make me care.

ROSA. How about your husband, your daughter, your family?

(**MANUELA** *starts to walk towards the garden. As she does, the dining room begins to dissolve.*)

MANUELA. I love them, but those buses are my reason, my future. My incentive, my job.

(**ROSA** *and* **MANUELA** *exit. We are now inside a tool shed located in the field where the buses are kept.* **MARIO** *is there with* **ANTONIO**, *who is eating a Cuban sandwich.*)

ANTONIO. You sure you don't want to sit where I'm sitting?

MARIO. Actually, I do.

ANTONIO. Sit – by all means – sit.

MARIO. I mean the chair is supposed to be for the management.

ANTONIO. Of course, perfectly understandable. I've been sitting all day long driving the bus anyway, I'm so glad I'm not the conductor anymore; that's a tough job, on your feet all day, having to deal with people all day.

MARIO. You have me to thank. I promoted you.

ANTONIO. Want a bite of my sandwich?

MARIO. No, I'm having lunch soon.

ANTONIO. I love the way cousin Manuela cooks. I might ask her to be the godmother to my baby, my wife wants her to be. My mother has missed the Sunday lunches. Will you be having one again soon, she wanted me to ask.

(**OSCAR** *enters.*)

OSCAR. Tell your mother on Mother's Day as usual.

ANTONIO. Thank you, Oscar. Can't wait. Want a bite of my sandwich?

OSCAR. I need you to fill up the number ten.

ANTONIO. Right. Yes, sir. My wife and I were wondering if you and cousin Manuela would like to baptize our baby? You're the best godfather I could think of for my baby – we'd really like that. My mother said you already have so many that you've baptized half of Guanabacoa...

OSCAR. I would love to. Now go.

ANTONIO. Thank you, sir.

(**ANTONIO** *exits.* **OSCAR** *goes to a box, unlocks it, and takes out a machine gun.*)

OSCAR. Why did you tell her?! Why do you always go behind my back?! Stop tricking me!

MARIO. She got it out of me. She knew already.

OSCAR. Liar!

MARIO. She tricked me.

OSCAR. Why? Haven't I been good to you? Haven't I treated you like a brother?

MARIO. You have.

OSCAR. Then why do you sabotage me?

MARIO. Because...

OSCAR. Because what?

MARIO. You overwhelm me.

OSCAR. You don't trust me.

MARIO. No, I don't.

OSCAR. From now on I give the orders and you follow. Understand?

MARIO. No. I have a right to give orders, also – to make decisions that concern us!

OSCAR. No, never!

MARIO. This is also mine!

OSCAR. When I let you, when I decide.

MARIO. No!

OSCAR. It's up to me!

MARIO. No more, no!

OSCAR. Don't fight me now, Mario, not now.

MARIO. Equal. I want it to be equal.

OSCAR. I'm the boss. *(He slaps* **MARIO***)* Understand?

MARIO. No.

*(***HUGO*** enters.)*

HUGO. Wow, a machine gun. A real one.

OSCAR. Yes, real. Want to learn how to shoot it?

HUGO. Yeah. Yes. Shit, yes.

OSCAR. Let's go. I'll show you.

HUGO. Really, Uncle Oscar?

OSCAR. Really.

(They start to exit.)

Coming, Mario?

MARIO. When I'm ready.

OSCAR. I hope you're ready soon.

(They exit. **MARIO** *tries not to follow* **OSCAR***, but then does. As* **MARIO** *goes, we see* **MANUELA** *with a bucket full of flowers she has been cutting. She enters the dining room.* **ROSA** *enters from the kitchen.)*

MANUELA. I want these flowers in the middle of the table.

ROSA. Is there enough room for flowers?

MANUELA. Yes, of course.

ROSA. It's important to you to look at flowers while you eat?

MANUELA. These ones I cut, take the bucket, put them in a vase.

ROSA. All right. *(She exits)*

MANUELA. I worked hard to be able to look at flowers when I eat. Worked hard to be able to do a lot of things. No one handed Oscar and me anything on any silver platter…

*(***ROSA*** enters with the flowers.)*

ROSA. What?

MANUELA. I wasn't talking to you.

ROSA. Who's here?

MANUELA. Myself, God.

(**ROSA** *starts to arrange the flowers.*)

Leave me alone for a minute.

ROSA. But –

MANUELA. They look fine.

(**ROSA** *exits.* **MANUELA** *takes a chair, sits, lights a ciga-rette, looks at the lighter.*

Worked hard, didn't I? Aren't you supposed to reward people for honest work?

(**MARIA JOSEFA** *enters.*)

MARIA JOSEFA. Starving. Light me one. One of mine, Lucky Strikes, I love American cigs.

(**MANUELA** *hands her the lighter.*)

MARIA JOSEFA. Silver, Heavy.

MANUELA. Yes.

MARIA JOSEFA. Who did it belong to?

MANUELA. Father, don't you remember? All the headaches when you gave this to me?

MARIA JOSEFA. After he was shot.

MANUELA. Yes.

MARIA JOSEFA. Right. Mario accused me of, well, his usual accusations - was insulted that I gave it to you and not him.

MANUELA. Jealous.

MARIA JOSEFA. Yes, acted hurt. When is she going to have lunch ready?

MANUELA. Another half an hour she said.

MARIA JOSEFA. Lazy girl, that girl is so lazy.

MANUELA. You're the one that treats her like she's your best friend, makes her think she doesn't have to follow orders.

MARIA JOSEFA. I have a soft heart.

MANUELA. Well, how can one discipline a best friend?

MARIA JOSEFA. If it's in half an hour, why has she set the table already? The water will get warm. The ice cubes will melt. Help get these pitchers into the refrigerator.

MANUELA. It doesn't matter. I have to get some air. I'm suffocating. *(She runs out)*

MARIA JOSEFA. Silver lighter...Warm water, cold food. That's what happens when you stop doing things for yourself.

*(**SONIA** enters.)*

SONIA. Is Mama all right?

MARIA JOSEFA. Aren't you going to give me a kiss?

SONIA. Mama looked like she was crying. Got angry at me and –

MARIA JOSEFA. Middle age, that's all.

SONIA. – screamed at me that I should help you keep the water cold.

MARIA JOSEFA. Forget it. It's useless to keep order in this house. Sit and talk to me.

SONIA. I'm hungry. When's lunch?

MARIA JOSEFA. Whenever Rosa feels like it.

SONIA. I thought I was late. I rushed here.

MARIA JOSEFA. No such thing as punctuality in this house. In and out, that's all. All day long, bus drivers, mechanics, friends. In and out. Why haven't they gotten an office?

SONIA. They wanted to keep it all with the family.

MARIA JOSEFA. "With the family" is different than in the house.

SONIA. Dad has an office for his other business.

MARIA JOSEFA. But still everything is handled out of this house, out of this dining room.

SONIA. Mama won't let go.

MARIA JOSEFA. Why should she? Neither will I. But I would have liked an office, a place to drive to, a desk. Counting money on the table where you eat corrupts the food. Pretty blouse.

SONIA. Thank you.

MARIA JOSEFA. The shorts, I don't approve of. What does your husband think about you crossing the street in these shorts?

SONIA. I haven't asked.

MARIA JOSEFA. Not ladylike.

SONIA. Grace Kelly wears shorts just like these and she's a princess.

MARIA JOSEFA. She was an actress first. Too short.

SONIA. Look at this handkerchief. Do you like it? The lettering?

MARIA JOSEFA. Now that's ladylike.

(**ROSA** *enters.*)

SONIA. Thank you. Hello, Rosa.

(**ROSA** *finishes setting the table.*)

ROSA. How's it look?

SONIA. Fine.

ROSA. Hmmm, smell something?

SONIA. What are we having?

ROSA. Shrimp with tomato, white rice.

SONIA. I like the way you make that.

MARIA JOSEFA. My recipe.

SONIA. Grandma!

MARIA JOSEFA. Isn't that right?

ROSA. Yes, of course. I have to make sure it doesn't burn.
(*She exits*)

SONIA. Hmmmm.

MARIA JOSEFA. We'd sit with whole tablecloths, big ones, and embroider, my mother and me.

SONIA. How exciting.

MARIA JOSEFA. Restful, not exciting.

SONIA. Well, yes, exciting was the wrong word.

MARIA JOSEFA. Whole tablecloths we'd embroider for tables bigger than this one. People had larger families then, common to see a table that sat thirty. Easily.

SONIA. This one sits fifteen.

MARIA JOSEFA. Small, her on one side, me on the other -

SONIA. I wish…

MARIA JOSEFA. That you could have been there?

SONIA. That we still had one of those tablecloths so I could study it, maybe copy it. Maybe you could remember the stitch. And Mama, you and I could sit on the front porch and embroider one for this table.

MARIA JOSEFA. Too late.

SONIA. No.

MARIA JOSEFA. I don't remember the stitches, the pattern, just remember that it was beautiful and people envied us.

SONIA. It might all come back to you.

MARIA JOSEFA. We got too busy for those things, your mother and I. Then one forgets.

SONIA. I've learned how to at school, but small things, towels, handkerchiefs –

MARIA JOSEFA. Your work, it's lovely.

SONIA. Nothing as monumental as a tablecloth but –

MARIA JOSEFA. I feel seasick, that's old age. Feeling like you're on a rocky sea in a little boat that goes up and down, side to side, nothing stable, all the time, even on a clear, cool, still day like this one. Light the cig for me?

(SONIA *lights it*)

Get one for yourself.

SONIA. I don't feel like it, thank you.

MARIA JOSEFA. Pregnant again?

SONIA. No.

MARIA JOSEFA. Never heard of a young woman turning

down a cigarette.

SONIA. Don't feel like one now, that's all. The table looks pretty, the flowers could use more careful arranging.

MARIA JOSEFA. You know Rosa, throws things together carelessly.

SONIA. Doesn't have any pride.

MARIA JOSEFA. No, she doesn't have a work ethic.

SONIA. *(Arranging flowers)* See, prettier, isn't it?

MARIA JOSEFA. Much.

SONIA. So hungry.

MARIA JOSEFA. Your husband?

SONIA. Having lunch at his mother's.

MARIA JOSEFA. Son?

SONIA. At school.

MARIA JOSEFA. So you have the whole afternoon to rearrange flowers, that's good.

SONIA. Papa and I are going to go shopping for a car.

MARIA JOSEFA. For whom?

SONIA. For me!

MARIA JOSEFA. For you?

SONIA. Yes.

MARIA JOSEFA. You've learned to drive?!

SONIA. Yes.

MARIA JOSEFA. How wonderful!

SONIA. I want a sports car, I think.

MARIA JOSEFA. Driving beats the hell out of embroidering.

(They start to laugh.)

SONIA. Maybe.

*(**MANUELA** enters.)*

MANUELA. Sonia, go tell Rosa to start serving.

MARIA JOSEFA. You have a problem?

*(**SONIA** exits.)*

MANUELA. No.

MARIA JOSEFA. You've been talking and walking around for the last hour like somebody who has a problem.

MANUELA. Headache, hot.

MARIA JOSEFA. Still getting them?

MANUELA. Still.

MARIA JOSEFA. Our bodies are our curse.

MANUELA. And our blessing.

MARIA JOSEFA. More a curse than a blessing.

MANUELA. Still.

MARIA JOSEFA. What?

MANUELA. We have no choice.

MARIA JOSEFA. Better to have been born a man, believe me.

MANUELA. To have a man's body and a woman's intelligence, that's the winning combination. *(She looks out the door)* Here they come.

(SONIA reenters.)

SONIA. She's almost ready.

MANUELA. Rosa, they're coming up the garden, Rosa, hurry up, you know Mario likes his food hot.

ROSA. *(Entering)* Burning, not just hot, burning! He doesn't think something is good unless it burns his tongue.

(SONIA sits.)

SONIA. Finally lunch.

MARIA JOSEFA. The men get served first.

SONIA. I know.

MARIA JOSEFA. We sit first, but they get served first.

MANUELA. She knows.

MARIA JOSEFA. Should I help you?

ROSA. Well.

MANUELA. No.

MARIA JOSEFA. Hugo coming for lunch?

MANUELA. He's with them.

(OSCAR, MARIO and HUGO enter.)

HUGO. Smells great!

ROSA. Shrimp and tomato. *(She enters and exits with food)*

MARIO. Great, who's going to serve me?

MARIA JOSEFA. I'll serve Oscar, Sonia, you serve your uncle…

HUGO. And me?

MANUELA. I will, nephew, it would be a pleasure.

ROSA. Here are some bananas.

MANUELA. Save some for yourself-

ROSA. Have a plate in the back.

OSCAR. Give me a kiss, sweetheart.

SONIA. Dad, well?

OSCAR. We'll have to see.

MANUELA. Don't tease her.

SONIA. I want something nice.

MARIA JOSEFA. A car.

MANUELA. Impressive, isn't it, Mama?

MARIA JOSEFA. Avocado for you, Oscar?

OSCAR. Two pieces.

MARIO. More, I'm starving.

SONIA. What else is new, Uncle?

HUGO. The bus drivers were acting strange today. One of them said goodbye.

(**ROSA** *exits to the front rooms.*)

SONIA. Maybe he's a Batistiano, maybe he's going to Miami to join the rest of them.

MANUELA. Yes, maybe.

MARIA JOSEFA. No talk against Batista in this house!

OSCAR. I'm beginning to miss Batista.

MARIA JOSEFA. How is it?

OSCAR. Good. Delicious.

MARIA JOSEFA. My recipe.

MANUELA. Oscar! Never mind. Mario, slow down when you're eating.

MARIO. I'm eating to keep myself from talking.

MANUELA. Then eat up!

MARIA JOSEFA. There's plenty more in the kitchen.

MANUELA. I know.

SONIA. And for the car.

OSCAR. Well...

SONIA. What kind of budget can I expect?

OSCAR. I took out what we can afford.

SONIA. Oh.

OSCAR. It's in my pockets.

SONIA. Oh.

OSCAR. A few bills.

SONIA. In your pocket?

OSCAR. Here, let's count it.

MANUELA. After lunch, surprises are better on a full stomach.

OSCAR. *(Taking out bills)* One thousand.

SONIA. My God!

OSCAR. Two thousand.

MARIO. Two thousand dollars in two bills.

OSCAR. That's right.

MARIO. Let me, let me look at it.

SONIA. Let him keep counting!

MARIO. Pesos, a thousand pesos.

OSCAR. A peso is worth eleven cents more than a dollar.

MANUELA. So there!

MARIA JOSEFA. Let me see the other one.

OSCAR. Here you go.

SONIA. I want to hold them in my hands, all of them, however many there are!

MARIA JOSEFA. *(Looking at bill)* What beautiful pieces of paper.

SONIA. They're for me, for my car! *(She giggles)*

MANUELA. Give them back to her.

MARIO. Spoiled.

MARIA JOSEFA. I'm glad she's spoiled.

HUGO. Unbelievable, how much more, Uncle Oscar, how much more?!

OSCAR. It's only money. Now… *(Takes out more bills)* three thousand, four thousand. For your new car.

SONIA. I'll be able to buy the sports car for sure now!

MANUELA. And keep the change.

HUGO. Let me hold it for a minute.

SONIA. No, it's mine. I love you, Papa. After lunch we'll go?

(ROSA reenters from the front rooms.)

ROSA. Sir, Mr. Oscar, there are three officials at the door.

OSCAR. We'll find the right car for you even if it takes all afternoon.

ROSA. Sir, I'm sorry to interrupt you, but three milicianos are at the front door. They have a document they want to give you. They wouldn't let me take it for you, they want you.

OSCAR. Tell them to wait till I'm through eating lunch.

ROSA. But sir…

OSCAR. Till I'm through eating lunch!

ROSA. Sir, madam, I'm scared of them.

MANUELA. I'll go talk to them.

(MANUELA and ROSA exit.)

OSCAR. Tell them to wait till after lunch!

SONIA. It's going to be red, a Karmann Ghia maybe, an MG. Or a Fiat. If it's a Fiat, I want it to be white. I like Karmann Ghias, I think they're more roomy, more subtle. If it's a Karmann Ghia, I think gray. The color gray, MG dark green, Fiat, white, but all of them with a black leather interior. Hold my money, Daddy, till we buy it.

HUGO. Let me hold it.

SONIA. No! I'll hold it, it's mine!

MARIA JOSEFA. I can't eat this! It's choking me! Can't eat it! Rosa!

SONIA. I'll give you a ride in it, Hugo.

HUGO. Can I drive it? Will you let me?

SONIA. Only if I'm in the car with you.

OSCAR. Mario, I am finishing my lunch! We are finishing lunch!

MARIO. Fine, what difference does it make?

MARIA JOSEFA. Rosa!

ROSA. I'm here, I'm coming, they haven't left.

OSCAR. Tell Manuela to come and start eating her lunch. It's getting cold.

MARIA JOSEFA. Take me to my room. I'm feeling faint. I can't eat.

ROSA. Yes, hold on to me.

> (**MARIA JOSEFA** *and* **ROSA** *exit.*)

MARIA JOSEFA. Thank you, you're a sweet girl.

SONIA. Can I be excused from lunch, I can't eat, I can't wait, I have to go show Osvaldo.

MARIO. Go out the side door.

SONIA. Why?

MARIO. Just do it!

SONIA. All right.

OSCAR. Tell your husband, next car I expect him to pay for.

SONIA. He will. See you in a minute. *(She exits)*

OSCAR. Good shrimp. Nice, Hugo, huh?

HUGO. Yes.

> (**MANUELA** *enters.*)

OSCAR. Now eat.

MANUELA. I don't want to.

OSCAR. Eat!

MANUELA. They read me the notice.

OSCAR. Not now, now we are eating.

MANUELA. They're taking them over after his speech to-night.

HUGO. What?

MANUELA. The buses.

MARIO. Let's burn them.

MANUELA. Never.

HUGO. What?

MANUELA. Fidel, he's getting rid of us.

HUGO. What?!

MANUELA. Leave the boy alone.

MARIA JOSEFA. One lily of the valley. It didn't mean one more year, one more month, it meant today, one more day for me to live.

MARIO. The old lady has gone crazy!

OSCAR. Shut up!

MARIA JOSEFA. My life...Just today left. Hold me, Manuela, hold me.

(**MANUELA** *goes toward* **MARIA JOSEFA**. **MARIA JOSEFA** *faints.*)

MANUELA. Fainted, don't go today, Mama, don't.

MARIO. Today, a day comes everything changes. Today.

OSCAR. No.

HUGO. Not everything.

OSCAR. I'll carry her to her room.

MANUELA. Yes.

HUGO. Not everything, Uncle Oscar!

(**OSCAR** *and* **MANUELA** *exit with* **MARIA JOSEFA**. **HUGO** *starts to cry.*)

MARIO. Stop it. Eat.

HUGO. How can you think of eating?

MARIO. Why not?

HUGO. Pervert!

MARIO. Watch it?

HUGO. Old –

MARIO. Careful!

HUGO. Why should I be careful?

MARIO. Might tell.

HUGO. About what?

MARIO. We're all in the same boat.

HUGO. No.

MARIO. Did you get a hard-on when he was counting the money?

HUGO. Faggot. He got yours up.

MARIO. You need someone older to teach you.

HUGO. You?

MARIO. Do you?

HUGO. You would help me? Have you always been?

MARIO. What I do with my fluids is my business.

HUGO. Are you always watching me?

MARIO. What I do with my eyes is my business.

HUGO. Well, I don't want you.

MARIO. Arm-wrestle with me, and this time, try to win.

HUGO. All right. I will.

(They start to arm-wrestle.)

MARIO. There's happiness, when everybody loses, a sense of justice, a sense of peace, so make me lose.

HUGO. I'm trying.

MARIO. Try harder!

(Blackout.)

END OF ACT ONE

ACT TWO

Scene 1

(The bus yard. On either side of the stage, there is the front of a bus. In the middle, open space. On the horizon, we see the garage. Late afternoon. **FULGENCIO**, *a man in his forties, and* **ANTONIO**, *in his twenties.)*

ANTONIO. Poor people.

FULGENCIO. They got quite a crowd.

ANTONIO. Father Beneficio passed out secret notes last night at the church.

FULGENCIO. I told every passenger last night to come and help the protest. First, they'll want to take over companies. Then they'll want to brainwash our children's minds. That's what Communists are like.

ANTONIO. They expect newspaper people here. From the U.S., maybe even CBS.

FULGENCIO. Who?

ANTONIO. Those are the people that do the Desi show.

FULGENCIO. How do I look?

ANTONIO. Good. Where are they?

FULGENCIO. The militia?

ANTONIO. Oscar – where is he?

FULGENCIO. Manuela is giving the crowd water, bless her.

ANTONIO. She's a good woman, my cousin.

FULGENCIO. Yes. I think Fidel is still going to get his way.

ANTONIO. Nah.

FULGENCIO. I'm just here to be counted.

*(**ROSA** and **MANUELA** enter. **ROSA** is carrying paper cups. **HUGO** follows them with a big bottle of water that's almost empty.)*

MANUELA. If they want civil disobedience, we'll give them civil disobedience.

ROSA. They love you, they were so happy you gave them water.

MANUELA. Well, they're helping us.

FULGENCIO. This is all very well organized.

ROSA. But you could have sent me. But no, you went there and gave them the water yourself and thanked them. They won't forget that act of generosity!

ANTONIO. Quite a woman, my cousin.

MANUELA. Fidel isn't going to ruin transportation without me putting up a fight.

HUGO. That's telling them, Auntie.

FULGENCIO. Where's Oscar?

MANUELA. Nobody can run these buses better than us. They don't belong to anyone but us.

FULGENCIO. People always said you had the cleanest buses in this country.

ROSA. That's why they've come to protest.

HUGO. I'll go and take the bottle back to the kitchen.

MANUELA. Wait, Hugo. Do you want a glass, Antonio? Fulgencio?

ANTONIO. Gotta admit my mouth's dry.

FULGENCIO. Why not?

ROSA. Here. I'll get it.

MANUELA. Quite a crowd.

ANTONIO. I thought it'd be bigger.

ROSA. Here, Fulgencio.

MANUELA. It's big enough. He wants to see masses of organized people working towards a common goal.

ROSA. Antonio?

ANTONIO. Thanks.

MANUELA. Well, Fidel Castro…

ROSA. Take it to the kitchen now, Hugo.

MANUELA. I'm going to show you how it's done.

HUGO. Right. *(He exits)*

FULGENCIO. Well, we're ready.

ANTONIO. Yeah, but we need some reassurance from your husband.

FULGENCIO. We're sort of letting our necks hang out waiting for the machete.

ROSA. We got to protect our lives.

FULGENCIO. Yes, that's what I'm saying.

MANUELA. He'll be here in a minute. Go and get him, Rosa –

ANTONIO. Has he been drinking?

ROSA. What do you think?

FULGENCIO. He must be.

ANTONIO. I know I would be.

MANUELA. My husband can handle whiskey. He's watching over my mother.

ANTONIO. Jesus save her soul!

ROSA. Amen!

MANUELA. You go take over, Rosa.

ROSA. I don't get to protest?

MANUELA. Someone has to be with Mama.

ROSA. Yes, God save her soul!

ANTONIO. Amen.

> *(**ROSA** exits.)*

More important to have the boss here than his maid.

FULGENCIO. That's for sure.

MANUELA. He's tense.

FULGENCIO. Of course.

ANTONIO. I know I would be also.

> *(**MARIO** enters.)*

MANUELA. How's Mama?

MARIO. The same.

ANTONIO. We're so sorry about that.

FULGENCIO. But she lived to be eighty. How many people can claim that?

MARIO. Unconscious to the fall of the bus empire.

ANTONIO. Always making a joke about everything.

MARIO. Why not?

ANTONIO. Respect your mother, at least your mother.

MARIO. Why?

ANTONIO. 'Cause of what she did for you. I respect mine and know the pain she went through to give me life. I can never, ever repay…

MARIO. Good. As long as you respect yours, why should you give a fuck about what I do with mine?

ANTONIO. Because I believe in a sense of decency.

MARIO. When did that start?

ANTONIO. Don't get me angry, Mario, or I'll…well, you won't know what hit you. I want respect for myself and my family members…

MARIO. What does that have to do with my mother and I?

FULGENCIO. She's his mother's cousin.

MARIO. Right.

ANTONIO. My mother thinks your mother is an angel.

MARIO. Well, she's not.

FULGENCIO. Don't upset him, he worships your family.

MARIO. Tell that to your mother.

ANTONIO. What I do today I'm doing for my fifth cousin Maria Josefa – not you, Mario – in her honor.

MARIO. I'm glad you have a reason.

ANTONIO. Want to go and fight it out?

FULGENCIO. This is not a time to fight among ourselves.

MARIO. Why not?

ANTONIO. I haven't forgotten the tricks you played on me when I was a kid!

MARIO. Good.

MANUELA. Will you two stop it!

ANTONIO. Sorry.

MARIO. Kiss my ass.

ANTONIO. Don't say those things in front of your sister.

MARIO. She knows…

MANUELA. Mario, please!

MARIO. She knows her mother said nothing when our father was shot right here. He was standing right here in this bus yard.

MANUELA. That was thirty years ago.

MARIO. Twenty-nine. I've kept an accurate account of everything – everything that's owed me.

MANUELA. Must be a big book you keep, brother.

MARIO. We never bothered to find out why he was shot, how, who shot him. We just kept the buses going for her husband.

MANUELA. For all of us.

MARIO. For you.

MANUELA. When I take a stand here today, maybe I'll pay you back a couple of pages – a couple of columns in your account book.

MARIO. No.

MANUELA. Help me! I need you to help me!

MARIO. So you two are with us, behind us!

ANTONIO. We'll lay down in front of the buses with you.

FULGENCIO. I brought my gun. *(He shows them)* Been wanting to use this baby for a long time.

MARIO. Good-looking gun.

FULGENCIO. Bought it from an ex-spy.

MARIO. American.

FULGENCIO. USA Marine.

MARIO. Impressive.

MANUELA. I don't think there should be any shooting. I think passive resistance. We lay in front of the buses. They're not going to drive over us. It wouldn't look good in the world press tomorrow. Those weird writers in France…

MARIO. Existentialists…

MANUELA. Yes, existentialists wouldn't like it.

FULGENCIO. Good.

ANTONIO. Strike – give them some of their own medicine.

FULGENCIO. I'll drive my car down the block, when I honk the horn three times, it means they're on their way.

MARIO. And the other bus drivers?

FULGENCIO. They refused to come with us.

ANTONIO. They said they'd drive their routes as if it were any ordinary day.

FULGENCIO. My feeling is that they'll try to confiscate these buses first and then go after the ones that are on routes.

MANUELA. As long as our protest is heard, we'll get our way.

FULGENCIO. See you soon.

MANUELA. Good.

ANTONIO. Where's cousin Oscar?

MARIO. Drinking.

MANUELA. Don't worry, he'll be here soon. He's with my mother, like I told you.

ANTONIO. I'm so sorry, Manuela, what a sad day.

MANUELA. Yes, well…

ANTONIO. She is a great woman.

MANUELA. Yes, she is.

ANTONIO. Too bad she has such an ungrateful son.

MARIO. Is that what your mother told you?

MANUELA. Leave him alone, Mario!

ANTONIO. Count on me. The other bus drivers said we were crazy to get involved, to help you. But I knew that it was my duty to help you. Is Hugo coming out?

MANUELA. Yes, of course.

ANTONIO. Good. We need all the men from the immediate family that we can get. No offence, Fulgencio.

FULGENCIO. We need more people, period.

MANUELA. More will show up.

MARIO. This won't work, sister.

MANUELA. Yes, It will. It's what we fought for – the right to protest.

MARIO. This is not a democracy anymore, sister.

MANUELA. We'll make it one again.

ANTONIO. Yes.

(**ANTONIO** and **FULGENCIO** exit.)

MANUELA. Why are you so bitter, Mario? Why can't you just help me?

MARIO. I'm tired.

MANUELA. Tired of me?

MARIO. Tired of picking up the crumbs he left on the floor for me.

MANUELA. Well, if we don't do something, there won't be any crumbs left to pick.

MARIO. Whoring my future, for your husband.

MANUELA. I'm glad you didn't say "for me."

MARIO. Now risking my life, the last favor.

MANUELA. "Favor?" He did you the favor. What were you? Struggling – struggling to get Father to give you a cent, working for him, having him control you, every word you said, everything you did, so he could run around with every married woman in Guanabacoa. You were his slave.

MARIO. You didn't have to work. You stayed at home and –

MANUELA. We were all Papa's slaves – slaves to his vanity, no business sense. This family had nothing. We were going nowhere, and then Oscar –

MARIO. Made us rich.

MANUELA. Yes.

MARIO. And our father was shot, and we pretended not to notice.

MANUELA. So we could get rich. And we did. Oscar kept his promise.

MARIO. Sometimes I despise you.

MANUELA. Your own sister?

MARIO. Yes.

MANUELA. And how do you think I feel about you? You think you made me feel proud, brother?

MARIO. You always act proud. Too proud for a woman.

MANUELA. Because of Oscar, he brought me pride.

(**HUGO** *enters.*)

HUGO. Are they here yet?

MARIO. No.

HUGO. I'm ready for anything.

MARIO. Are you going to go galloping on your horse?

HUGO. Come on!

MANUELA. Leave him alone.

MARIO. No, you'd want to protect her, her you wouldn't want to give up. The horse is the only real love of his life.

HUGO. What's wrong with that?

MANUELA. Look, Hugo, you lay in front of number three, Mario, you in front of the six. Oscar, in front of the nine. I'll be in front of this one, the ten. Antonio, five. Fulgencio, the two.

HUGO. Yes.

MARIO. Good.

HUGO. What's good?

MARIO. We have another enemy now.

HUGO. Besides Batista.

MARIO. Besides ourselves.

MANUELA. Go and do it.

(**MARIO** *and* **HUGO** *exit.*)

It will work. There is justice in the world. There is. I still believe in it. The number ten, bought six years ago. *(She goes to the bus)* My life.

*(**OSCAR** enters with a machine gun.)*

OSCAR. Come on! Sons of bitches! Come on!

MANUELA. Oscar, no!

OSCAR. I'm a man! I fight like a man!

MANUELA. No, please!

OSCAR. The fight is all that matters.

MANUELA. No, what matters is not losing.

OSCAR. Come on, I'm ready for you! Sons of bitches! Reds! Assholes!

MANUELA. You're going to throw yourself in front of that bus over there, the number nine.

OSCAR. I'm going to fight! I'm going to show them that Oscar Hernandez has balls made out of steel, what fighting a man with steel balls is all about.

MANUELA. You're drunk, Oscar. This is not the time to get drunk.

OSCAR. Sometimes a drink is just the courage you need… Just the fuel you need so you can function, like these buses and gasoline.

MANUELA. We're throwing ourselves in front of the buses so the world can hear us.

OSCAR. No, an eye for an eye, testicle for a testicle, dream shattered for dream shattered. Blood!

MANUELA. We're going to throw ourselves in front of the bus. I, in front of this one! You, in front of that one!

OSCAR. No, fight! *(To machine gun)* Yes, baby?

MANUELA. That's not the way.

*(We hear a car horn honk three times. **MANUELA** lies in front of the bus.)*

Three times, that means they are on their way up the hill.

OSCAR. No, I don't like you on the ground. I don't like seeing my wife in dirt!

MANUELA. Put the machine gun inside the garage, and lie down in front of your bus.

OSCAR. The man I am is the property that I have acquired. That is Oscar Hernandez, the acreage, the boats, the tractors, the fleet of buses, the machinery and now –

MANUELA. You're going to lie on the ground and let the world know what they're doing to you. And we will be able to keep it all.

OSCAR. Without them, I'm an orphan.

(**HUGO** *enters.*)

A fool.

HUGO. They're here. They started on Antonio's.

MANUELA. Hide the machine gun, Oscar!

(**OSCAR** *runs out.*)

Go to your bus, Hugo.

HUGO. I have time.

MANUELA. Don't be scared.

HUGO. All right.

MANUELA. This will work. There are working people everywhere in the world. They understand what owning something means to a person. How it makes life bearable. How it makes you have something to leave behind to your children. In the United States, that's what their society is founded on, the right to advance yourself, the right to own something, and they won't let this happen to us. They'll help us.

HUGO. They'll send in the fleet!

MANUELA. Yes!

HUGO. I'm sorry. I don't know why 1 believed in him, Fidel, I needed…

MANUELA. By tomorrow afternoon the news of our struggle to keep what belongs to us will have spread all over the world. We'll be in the *New York Times*! And the owners of all the small businesses that keep the world from going bankrupt, that keep people from starving, will be on our side and we will win, Hugo!

HUGO. (*He looks out into the street*) They are trying to drive the first two away.

MANUELA. Fulgencio's and Antonio's?

HUGO. Mario's and mine they'll try next.

MANUELA. Go, Hugo, time to be a man.

> (**HUGO** *runs out.* **OSCAR** *enters. We hear the crowd cheering.*)

OSCAR. Fight!

MANUELA. They're all with us.

OSCAR. Of course. People love me in this town. We're going to win.

MANUELA. Fight them!

OSCAR. Yes, *(He lies down in front of the other bus)* Thank you, Manuela, for making me see.

MANUELA. Don't thank me.

OSCAR. You're so much better than me.

MANUELA. For thirty years you have been my reason.

OSCAR. Your reason?

MANUELA. My reason, for everything in life.

> (*We hear two buses being driven away. Fumes start to come onto the stage.*)

> (*Coughing*) What is that?

OSCAR. Fumes.

MANUELA. They took two of them.

OSCAR. Cowards!

MANUELA. I knew I couldn't trust them.

> (**ANTONIO** *runs in.*)

ANTONIO. They had a gun to my head!

MANUELA. You should have stayed!

ANTONIO. They were going to pull the trigger.

MANUELA. No! They're not going to kill a worker.

ANTONIO. I could tell!

MANUELA. Did they?

ANTONIO. I could tell they were planning to. Who would have fed my wife and the baby? I have to think of them.

MANUELA. You let them drive the bus away.

ANTONIO. Yes, the two of them.

MANUELA. Fulgencio also?

ANTONIO. Fulgencio didn't even lay down.

MANUELA. What!

ANTONIO. He ran. They drove off before he had a chance to lay down. At least I laid down.

MANUELA. For two minutes!

ANTONIO. That's long enough to see your life running past you, and I haven't had a life yet, except for my wife and the baby.

MANUELA. I guess you're not really family.

ANTONIO. I am!

MANUELA. The family is still laying down.

ANTONIO. Manuela, respect me.

MANUELA. Why?

OSCAR. Coward!

ANTONIO. I respect, love the both of you.

MANUELA. Not enough to go down with us.

OSCAR. Smell it, smell the gasoline.

ANTONIO. I know what gasoline smells like.

OSCAR. Smell my hands, this gasoline is me, it's in my pores.

(*We hear two buses drive away.*)

ANTONIO. Well, the family just let go of two more buses.
(*We hear the crowd cheering.*)

MANUELA. Why are they cheering?

OSCAR. The crowd must be throwing things at the buses.

ANTONIO. I don't think so.

OSCAR. I know so. The people of this town look up to me. I've been good to them.

ANTONIO. People forget.

MANUELA. You and I, Oscar, we will not budge!

OSCAR. Till the newspapers get here.

MANUELA. And we'll win.

ANTONIO. Don't kill yourself for this, what's a bus? What's a business if you got yourselves, if you love…

(**OSCAR** and **MANUELA** start to laugh.)

Don't laugh at me.

MANUELA. A business becomes who you are.

OSCAR. This bus, is me.

ANTONIO. You're both losing your minds.

MANUELA. Every day your work becomes who you are.

OSCAR. Who we are.

(**MARIO** enters with two milicianos.)

MARIO. Here they are, the owners.

MANUELA. Traitor!

MARIO. Why fight the future?

MANUELA. The future!

MARIO. They would have run me over.

ANTONIO. See, I told you they're intending to kill us.

MILICIANO 1. We would not…

MARIO. You got close.

MILICIANO 2. That's all.

MILICIANO 1. Testing you.

MARIO. I don't like threats.

MILICIANO 1. Now you two get up.

MANUELA. Never. Never!

OSCAR. I'm a man who listens to his wife.

MILICIANO 2. Fuck, here we go again.

MANUELA. Have other people revolted in this way?

MILICIANO 1. Only here, everybody else handed them over with dignity.

MANUELA. What do you know about dignity?

MILICIANO 2. Watch it, lady.

ANTONIO. Be careful, Manuela!

MILICIANO 1. I'm going to ask nicely once. Then we're going to take you off to jail. There's a mob forming outside.

MANUELA. See, what did I tell you. Good!

MILICIANO 1. All along the street. They're going quite out of control.

OSCAR. That's the idea.

MILICIANO 1. We're trying to keep them from coming in and harming you.

OSCAR. Harming us. Ha!

MARIO. They're yelling, "Take them, take the buses from those imperialist pigs!"

MANUELA. Stop your teasing.

MILICIANO 2. If you people would just listen, maybe you'd learn something.

MILICIANO 1. Shut up, Paco! Listen.

(We hear the mob yelling "Take them. Take them!")

OSCAR. I don't believe it.

MANUELA. Greedy, everybody's so greedy.

MILICIANO 1. So let's do this peacefully.

MANUELA. No.

OSCAR. I refuse!

MANUELA. *(Shouting)* We refuse you sons of bitches! Daughters of whores!

MILICIANO 1. Jesus.

MILICIANO 2. Oh God…

MILICIANO 1. Why did I get stuck with this?

MILICIANO 2. 'Cause you believe in the good of the revolution…

MILICIANO 1. Right.

MARIO. I told you, owners are owners. Hard to let go.

ANTONIO. Whose side are you on?

MARIO. My own!

MILICIANO 1. Please ma'am, sir, we've already confiscated all the others.

OSCAR. I don't believe you.

MILICIANO 1. The ones that were on their daily routes, the bus drivers just handed over.

MILICIANO 2. Willingly.

ANTONIO. At least I didn't do that.

MANUELA. Shut up, Antonio, not now!

MARIO. You will.

ANTONIO. No, I'll never drive a bus for them.

MARIO. Wait and see…

ANTONIO. Only 'cause I have to feed my family. What am I supposed to do? I don't have thousands buried anywhere…

MILICIANO 1. We got only these two buses left to confiscate.

MANUELA. Steal!

MILICIANO 1. So please, let us do it peacefully. I don't want to put two old people in jail.

OSCAR. Kill us first.

MILICIANO 1. Get in his bus.

MILICIANO 2. Yes, fine. Plan three?

MILICIANO 1. Yes, plan three.

MARIO. They're all turned against us, sister.

MANUELA. Leave us alone, Mario!

MILICIANO 1. Drive for fucking Christ sake!

ANTONIO. There's a lady here, my cousin, enough, enough!

(**MILICIANO** *2 puts the bus that* **OSCAR** *is lying in front of into reverse and drives off.*)

OSCAR. Oh my God! We didn't think about reverse!

MARIO. Pretty smart for a bunch of morons.

MILICIANO 1. Who's a moron?

MARIO. You!

OSCAR. No, not them, us. *(He gets up, starts to walk away)*

MILICIANO 1. *(Pointing at* **ANTONIO***)* Now you.

ANTONIO. Antonio…

MANUELA. Oscar, Oscar, where are you going?

OSCAR. To die.

MARIO. To drink.

ANTONIO. My name is Antonio, and you know 'cause I used to date your sister.

MILICIANO 1. I thought you looked familiar.

MANUELA. Don't leave me, Oscar.

OSCAR. Get up and join me.

MANUELA. Get on the other side of the bus!

MILICIANO 1. Antonio, get on the bus and drive it away.

(**OSCAR** *exits.*)

ANTONIO. Forgive me, my dear cousin Manuela. *(He exits)*

MANUELA. How about honor, Antonio?

MARIO. Honor? When did anybody in this family have honor?

(**SONIA** *runs in.*)

SONIA. Mama, she's awake, the yelling in the street woke Grandma up, she's not dying, it's a miracle, a sign.

MANUELA. A trick.

MARIO. I'll tell Mama the bad news.

MANUELA. No, let her die happy, let her die successful.

MARIO. All right.

MANUELA. Don't gloat!

MILICIANO 1. Drive!

(**MANUELA** *gets up and opens the hood of the bus. She lights her cigarette lighter.*)

MANUELA. I'm going to throw it in and blow it up!

SONIA. Mama, no! Please! No!

(**MILICIANO 1** *grabs* **MANUELA**)

MARIO. It wouldn't have worked, sister.

MILICIANO 1. Don't kick, lady!

MANUELA. Bastards!

MILICIANO 1. I was doing my job.

MANUELA. Faggot, killer, rapist!

MILICIANO 1. If you were a man, well, you wouldn't walk

out alive! *(He walks away)*

MANUELA. Scum!

MILICIANO 1. *(Yelling to her)* There's a place for you here. You could have a job running the buses. We'd pay you a fair wage. If you want it, work for the people, for mankind!

MANUELA. Up yours!

(We hear ANTONIO drive the last bus away and a crowd applauding.)

Beggars, greedy beggars!

SONIA. I'm sorry, Mama, I'm...

MANUELA. Let them tell me to my face.

SONIA. Where are you going, Mama?

MANUELA. Hugo, stop hiding behind that tree. They're gone.

HUGO. I'm sorry.

MANUELA. Why? You acted just like the other men in this family.

HUGO. Forgive me.

MANUELA. I don't forgive them, that crowd.

HUGO. Auntie, I'll go with you...

MANUELA. No, Mario and I.

MARIO. Yes, sister.

MANUELA. Let's make them look at us.

HUGO. They're happy 'cause the buses belong to them now.

MANUELA. They resented every nickel they ever had to pay.

(MARIO and MANUELA exit.)

SONIA. Hugo, don't go.

HUGO. Let's go back in.

SONIA. I can't yet. I don't want to see Papa like that. Stay with me, Hugo.

HUGO. Yes.

SONIA. It's empty; for the first time in my life, this field is empty.

HUGO. Sonia, did you know, did you think this was going to happen?

SONIA. Yes.

HUGO. How?!

SONIA. Osvaldo heard about it a month ago. I didn't want to believe it.

HUGO. Why isn't your husband here now?

SONIA. Osvaldo thinks he has enough tragedies just dealing with his family, that I should deal with mine.

HUGO. Who would believe it!

SONIA. I believe it. I believe it now.

HUGO. I don't want to believe it.

SONIA. In my car, last night, by myself…I drove along the beach, speeded…

HUGO. How much?

SONIA. Seventy miles an hour.

HUGO. Wow, that's great for a girl!

SONIA. Yeah, it felt…

HUGO. Powerful.

SONIA. Why am I telling you this?

HUGO. 'Cause I'm your favorite cousin.

SONIA. You're so young.

HUGO. No, I understand about speeding. Sometimes I ride my horse at night down the beach. I'm high up. Tall. And we gallop so fast, nothing like seventy miles, but fast. Sometimes I think it's going to kill the horse, but I push her! Still a horse is not like a car, not private enough…1 mean, the horse is there with you and she's an animal with some senses like your own, not a cold machine with no personality or mind. Indifferent. Must be something to be alone with an automobile.

SONIA. I thought I could escape.

HUGO. Escape what?

SONIA. My upbringing. Myself.

HUGO. Oh…why?

SONIA. So I could find…

HUGO. Excitement.

SONIA. A braver me. The other me…

HUGO. Two of you? I wouldn't want two of me. I've plenty to handle with one. Wait, I'll show you what Uncle Oscar taught me. *(He exits)*

SONIA. A daring me. The me that's a woman, not a child. I'm thirty years old. When does my family start? When do I become the mother? 1 thought when the baby was born it would happen but it didn't. Hugo? Hugo, where are you?!

*(***HUGO*** runs in with the machine gun.)*

HUGO. This is power – speeding in a car and shooting this!

SONIA. Don't, Hugo! They'll come hack and arrest us!

(He pretends he's going to pull the trigger.)

Please, Hugo, no!

(Hugo makes the sound of a machine gun.)

HUGO. See, no bullets! Couldn't find the bullets.

*(***MANUELA*** enters.)*

MANUELA. Put that away, Hugo.

HUGO. Sure. Sorry, Auntie, just having fun.

MANUELA. Pretending to be brave?

HUGO. Yes.

MANUELA. Pretense is over.

HUGO. Yes, Auntie. *(He exits)*

SONIA. What did they do?

MANUELA. They left.

SONIA. They didn't apologize?

MANUELA. They looked away. Without remorse.

SONIA. I thought you said this would work. We have nothing now, Mama.

MANUELA. I thought I knew what this country was about

– what people wanted.

SONIA. You believed in the good of people. You and Papa have always been too giving.

MANUELA. Is that what your husband told you?

SONIA. Yes.

MANUELA. He's probably right.

SONIA. Seems to be.

MANUELA. You should turn to him more.

SONIA. I think I should. *(She exits)*

MANUELA. *(To herself)* Oscar, you gave up.

*(**MARIO** enters.)*

MARIO. Papa died here. We covered it up. Pretended it didn't happen so we could get somewhere. Now it's all gone.

MANUELA. I don't know how to start. I don't know how to start again. Your little girl is scared. This is all I know. *(She starts to weep)* No, I won't. *(She stops crying)*

MARIO. Good, let's go and see how Mama's doing.

MANUELA. No, I'll sit here till I can figure out a way to forgive Oscar. I hope I can. Look at it. It's empty.

(She looks around. He walks to another side of the field.)

MARIO. They found your body here, Papa. Someone had shot you through the back.

(Blackout.)

Scene 2

(Lights up. Later. The dining room. **MARIO** *and* **SONIA** *are with* **MARIA JOSEFA**, *who is in a white nightgown and sitting on a chair.* **ROSA** *is bringing in a bowl of soup for* **HUGO**, *who starts to eat it.)*

MARIA JOSEFA. The world was so out of reach.

MARIO. And the other side?

MARIA JOSEFA. Unreal also, like sunrise in a desert.

MARIO. What desert, Mama, you've never been in a fucking desert!

ROSA. Don't scream at her. She's weak –

HUGO. He wants to…

MARIO. To what?!

HUGO. Never mind!

MARIA JOSEFA. The desert of my heart, of my soul, of my longing, not tangible. Cold, I feel so goddamned cold. I don't want to start shuddering again. I don't want to shake from the cold! I hate refrigerators!

SONIA. Change of body temperature. Is that a sign, Uncle?

ROSA. Don't bury her yet!

MARIO. Who knows?

HUGO. We should call the doctor.

MARIO. What for? He told us to give her her last rites last night.

MARIA JOSEFA. I don't want the last morning of my life to be so cold. My feet are freezing, going numb.

HUGO. Frostbite.

MARIA JOSEFA. I don't know. Rub Mama's feet, Mario.

MARIO. Yes.

MARIA JOSEFA. See how you really love me -

*(***MARIO*** *is rubbing her feet.)*

Girl, get me a brandy like in the old days.

ROSA. Yes, Maria Josefa, yes.

MARIA JOSEFA. And one for yourself.

ROSA. Thank you.

MARIA JOSEFA. Let me feel something in my feet.

HUGO. Where's Auntie?

SONIA. Still sitting out on the field.

HUGO. Oh.

MARIA JOSEFA. Caress my feet. It snows in Spain. My husband, your father, he knew cold up there in the mountains. He was a monument, your father, a monument to manhood. None of you came close.

ROSA. Here, you need some help.

MARIA JOSEFA. I can drink a glass of brandy on my own!

ROSA. Thank you, Lord, for answering my prayer.

MARIA JOSEFA. I've only known two real men in my life...

MARIO. Really.

MARIA JOSEFA. Your father and Oscar Hernandez, the taxicab driver, Estrella's cousin...

SONIA. Grandma, you don't mean that.

MARIA JOSEFA. I do.

MARIO. Well, that real man disintegrated today.

HUGO. Shut up, Uncle Mario!

MARIA JOSEFA. Oscar, never! Never!

MARIO. He let them take your beloved-

(**OSCAR** *enters.*)

SONIA. Shut up!

OSCAR. Let him. Do it, Mario.

(*He pours himself shots of whiskey, at least three, and gulps them down silently*)

MARIO. All right.

SONIA. Uncle Mario, please don't. She's dying.

MARIO. Why shouldn't she know?

SONIA. For me. Don't tell her for me, for my sake.

MARIO. Two real men. What was I?

MARIA JOSEFA. A weakling. A weakling and a pervert.

HUGO. Even she knows.

ROSA. Hugo, shut up!

MARIO. Die alone, Mama.

MARIA JOSEFA. I'm not going to die. My drink has given me energy. Death was so like life, out of reach…a dream, not tangible, not…

MARIO. Die alone. Die without my love.

SONIA. Is she dead?

(**ROSA** *goes to* **MARIA JOSEFA.**)

ROSA. Asleep. Maybe she'll recover.

MARIO. The sugar's gone to the brain already. You heard the doctor's explanation.

ROSA. He also said she was never going to wake up!

(**MARIA JOSEFA** *wakes up again.*)

MARIA JOSEFA. The only thing tangible I ever had in my life was my husband. My husband on top of me, at my breast, biting it…

SONIA. Grandma, please stop, please.

ROSA. She's delirious.

HUGO. Uncle Oscar, can I borrow your car?

OSCAR. They took it. They took the car also.

HUGO. Did they take yours, Sonia?!

SONIA. No. Mine is safe at my husband's house.

MARIA JOSEFA. With me, in me. I needed him so much that I began to hate him. And the hate grew to bitterness and contempt and he was killed. I thought this morning he'd walk and greet me at heaven's door, but no, he wasn't there… Who are you fucking around with in heaven, husband?

HUGO. It's true. I hear Grandpa was a real stud, that somebody's husband shot him.

MARIO. All lies.

MARIA JOSEFA. What trollop has you occupied the day of my death! The day of our reunion?

OSCAR. All lost.

MARIA JOSEFA. Oscar Hernandez. Oscar, you greet me, you hold me.

(**OSCAR** *goes to hold her.* **MARIA JOSEFA** *falls asleep.*)

OSCAR. Tell your daughter to love me. Go outside and get her in here.

MARIO. She's asleep, Oscar, asleep…

HUGO. I'll go and get her. *(He runs out)*

MARIO. Come here, Oscar. Come sit by me. I'm awake.

(**OSCAR** *goes and weeps in his arms.*)

Cry, Oscar, yes. That's good. In my arms. Yes, weep. Good. Wonderful, wonderful for me to be the person that you've turned to, that you have let the grief go with me. Yes, rest, sigh, breathe…

OSCAR. But…

MARIO. No, no buts. This moment is ours, just you and I, us, together. Me comforting you, you needing me.

OSCAR. Now Manuela knows that I am a coward.

ROSA. Sonia, can I get you some soup?

SONIA. Yes, thank you.

ROSA. Fan your grandmother.

SONIA. Yes.

(**SONIA** *fans* **MARIA JOSEFA**. **ROSA** *goes into the kitchen.*)

MARIO. She doesn't know you. She's married to you and I thank God that you chose her, that you married my sister because that's how I became your family. But she didn't see you like I saw you. She didn't charge the passengers while you drove the bus. She wasn't at the gatherings when you spoke so eloquently of the future, and the future you spoke of came to pass and everything you promised happened.

OSCAR. And now it's gone.

MARIO. It'll never be gone.

OSCAR. How, Mario?!

MARIO. Because you in 1935, you in 1946, you in 1954, will always be alive in my mind. "Oscar the Conqueror" is what I'll have them put on your grave.

MARIA JOSEFA. *(Waking up)* Come over here, Oscar. Please be with me. Why are you crying, Oscar? Has someone died?

OSCAR. No.

MARIA JOSEFA. Are you in love with another woman?

OSCAR. Never.

MARIA JOSEFA. My daughter, does she make you truly happy?

OSCAR. Yes.

MARIA JOSEFA. Then you are crying with joy.

OSCAR. Yes. Joy that you are still alive. That I became, built, have a place in this family.

MARIA JOSEFA. I always felt safe with you, Oscar. Always so strong.

MARIO. Strong, Mama? If he's so strong, why was he crying in my arms?

SONIA. Papa. Papa, please, when is Mama going to come in? Go get her, please.

OSCAR. No.

SONIA. Please.

OSCAR. She'll come in when she understands…

SONIA. Understands what, Papa?

OSCAR. That we are what they want to throw away.

SONIA. No!

OSCAR. Understand that, Sonia.

SONIA. I don't want to…

MARIO. Oscar. I know how to save us.

OSCAR. Yes, comrades, you and I…

MARIA JOSEFA. And how, how did Manuela make you the happiest?

OSCAR. When she saw who she thought I was, which was so much better than the real me.

(MANUELA and HUGO enter.)

MANUELA. That's true.

MARIO. Leave him alone.

MANUELA. I thought you like cruelty in the family.

MARIO. I love him, like a brother.

MANUELA. Liar.

MARIO. You're not a man. Trying to understand, run in a man's world, but never could.

MANUELA. Poor Mama. You're not dead.

MARIA JOSEFA. Of course not.

MANUELA. I wish you were.

MARIA JOSEFA. How dare you!

(ROSA enters.)

ROSA. The soup, Sonia. I heated it up.

SONIA. Thank you.

(SONIA sits to eat. MANUELA walks over to MARIA JOSEFA.)

MARIA JOSEFA. My recipe.

MANUELA. You haven't told her?

OSCAR. Of course not.

MANUELA. Why didn't you, Mario?

MARIO. Couldn't do that to Oscar.

MANUELA. Liar, you're capable of anything.

MARIA JOSEFA. What are you talking about?

MARIO. Usual stuff, Mama.

MANUELA. Don't be coy. You know why Oscar is so drunk, Mama? 'Cause he should have told you....Our buses –

MARIA JOSEFA. Told me you make him happy. Aren't you the lucky one?

SONIA. I'm leaving.

HUGO. Take me with you.

SONIA. All right.

HUGO. We'll go for a ride, take it up to eighty.

SONIA. Good. If Osvaldo comes by here, tell him Hugo and I went racing.

MARIA JOSEFA. She shouldn't race without her husband!

ROSA. Yes, I'll tell him. Be careful.

(*They exit.*)

OSCAR. Cruel wife…You've turned cruel.

MARIO. Oscar, pour yourself a drink and one for me and let's toast to the past, to our past, glorious…Enough stories to tell to fill up the rest of your life.

OSCAR. I don't want the old lady to die unhappy.

MARIO. She won't believe her.

MANUELA. Mama, God wanted you to stay alive so I could tell you one last thing, so you could learn an important lesson before you leave this earth. In the end, all the years of struggle, the greed, the need, the work, the constant preoccupation with profit, future product –

OSCAR. Success, goddamnit! All we wanted was to be successful.

ROSA. Can I get anybody anything?

MANUELA. In the end…

MARIO. Have a break for the rest of your life.

ROSA. No, I like it here.

MANUELA. In the end, Mama, it wasn't worth it. They're gone, our buses are gone. The new government confiscated them. They own them now. They're no longer ours. We no longer own a business, Mama!

MARIA JOSEFA. What did I tell you about men with beards?! What did I tell you?!

MANUELA. No more business, no more country, no more profits.

MARIA JOSEFA. And you did nothing.

MANUELA. I threw myself in front of the bus.

ROSA. Good for you.

MARIO. But it didn't work.

MARIA JOSEFA. Go and get them back, Oscar.

OSCAR. I can't. He's crippled me. Fidel won. There's nothing I can do. I can't move. I'm frozen here.

MARIA JOSEFA. Rosa!

ROSA. What do you want, ma'am?

MARIA JOSEFA. To go to my room to die.

ROSA. Yes, ma'am.

(They start to exit.)

Aren't any of you coming?

MARIA JOSEFA. I want Mario.

MARIO. Only if you tell me that I am as much of a man as anybody else.

MARIA JOSEFA. Unfortunately, son, you are.

MARIO. And you love me.

MARIA JOSEFA. All mothers love their children.

OSCAR. I have to vomit, the drinks, I have to…

MARIO. In a moment. I'll go in, in a moment.

*(**MARIA JOSEFA** gestures that that is fine as **ROSA** helps her to her bedroom.)*

OSCAR. I gotta run…I gotta vomit.

MANUELA. If you have to vomit, vomit on my lap but stay here with me. Go on, Mario. Do it. Betray him now.

MARIO. Papa died. Was it an accident? A political move? Did you order it? Who will ever know. But I do know that you used it to take control of the business. To take it away from the family so you could have it for yourselves – That's all I'm doing using this opportunity for myself. It's fair. It's fair after all these years.

OSCAR. What are you talking about?

MANUELA. They offered him a job.

OSCAR. Who?

MANUELA. Fidel…

OSCAR. Who told you?

MANUELA. Antonio, when he came to pick up his tool box, he told me that everybody had to make a living…et cetera, et cetera, et cetera… and with his last et cetera he told me what a traitor you've turned into, brother.

Now Fidel is your savior. He's going to let you pretend to be my husband. Was he lying, Mario?

MARIO. No. Not Fidel, exactly, no. One of his men offered me the job. But...

OSCAR. You said no, of course, good boy. You've always been a good boy.

MARIO. Manager. Managing the buses. Regular income.

OSCAR. Bastards thinking you'd betrayed me. Filthy bastards.

MANUELA. He has betrayed you.

OSCAR. No, the family sticks together. You always underestimated your brother.

MANUELA. You're taking the job?

MARIO. Yes. I am.

(**OSCAR** *pushes* **MANUELA** *aside and grabs* **MARIO** *by his shirt collar.* **MANUELA** *sits down and lights a cigarette.*)

OSCAR. Justice is on my side! Justice! You fucking queer! Bastard!

(**OSCAR** *starts to hit* **MARIO**. **MARIO** *begins to shake.*)

MARIO. I'll have them arrest you. They're coming in...in a few minutes. I'm giving them the books, so they know how much money we make.

(**SONIA** *enters. She is hysterical.*)

SONIA. Mama! My car! They came for it! Osvaldo was going to hand it over to them 'cause it was in your name. Because it wasn't really mine.

MANUELA. Forget about it.

OSCAR. I'm gonna kill you. Right out there. Two shots and you're taken care of.

MARIO. Like my father?

OSCAR. Shut up!

SONIA. *(To* **MANUELA***)* And Hugo said the time to fight is now! And he got in the car, the milicianos started shooting at him, and Hugo smashed my car against the wall.

MANUELA. Is he all right? Have they shot him...oh God...

MARIO. That boy would pick the wrong time to be heroic.

SONIA. They arrested him.

MARIO. Let him spend the night in jail, it'll do him good.

SONIA. Osvaldo is trying to get Hugo out of jail. He's really angry at me. I always get into marital problems because of my family. Mama, I thought it was my car, but it wasn't. Why isn't anything mine?

MANUELA. 'Cause you haven't earned it.

*(During this, **OSCAR** has been looking for a gun. He finds one. He begins to load it.)*

OSCAR. Osvaldo should learn how to use a gun.

SONIA. Jesus, Jesus! You're all as crazy as Hugo…Jesus!

OSCAR. Manuela! Sonia! Under the table!

*(**SONIA** and **MANUELA** drop to the ground and start to crawl under the table.)*

I want you.

MARIO. Drop the gun. There is such a thing as law! Don't you fear the law?

OSCAR. A bullet. That's the law in this country…Always been…*(He aims but can't shoot)*…My hands are shaking…

MARIO. Too much booze. Don't lose all of your dignity, please, Oscar. You had so much dignity…I loved and hated you so…I can tell you now. I loved and hated you more than anything, more than my own life. Do you understand? …You must have known …. Do you know what it's been like to live just outside, so near but at the same time so apart …

OSCAR. Apart from what?

MARIO. Business, the family, business.

*(**OSCAR** shoots in the air. **SONIA** screams. **MANUELA** gets up. **ROSA** enters.)*

ROSA. She's asleep. Don't wake her up. I want her to die in her sleep like she deserves.

MANUELA. You scared the hell out of Sonia. Oscar, hand

me the gun.

(**OSCAR** *hands her the gun.*)

Mario, you betrayed a man whose only crime was wanting to help you.

OSCAR. I'm going to Fidel. I'm going to tell him exactly what I think of him. What a liar he's been. That all he is, is a liar.

MANUELA. I'm going with you.

MARIO. They'll arrest both of you.

OSCAR. They've already killed me. They can't do anything else.

MANUELA. Take me with you.

OSCAR. Of course

MANUELA. Through it all, together. He and I, Mario, together. Married. Blood really mixing with blood. Look at Sonia. That's Oscar and I, blessed by God.

MARIO. Fidel is the first chance I've ever had to be the boss.

ROSA. Working for Fidel, not boss. Like when Manuela let me decide what pot I wanted to buy for the rice. I got to pick it. Still, it didn't belong to me.

MARIO. We all own everything now. All equals.

SONIA. I'm sitting in the room with Grandma. I'm gonna pray for all of us. Prayer in moments like this is the only salvation. Put it all in Jesus' hands. Right, Rosa?

ROSA. Right, don't let her wake up...

SONIA. Thank you, Rosa. (*She goes to the bedroom*)

MANUELA. Because I was a woman, I was supposed to be weak? You hated me because I developed a mind. 'Cause I had a business sense. I could seduce Oscar and run our empire.

OSCAR. Let's go.

MANUELA. Here, Rosa. Bury this somewhere.

(*She hands* **ROSA** *the gun*)

ROSA. Be careful. Please, be careful.

MARIO. What good is your business sense going to do you in jail?

MANUELA. I'll plan our revenge. It isn't over yet, Mario. Not yet.

OSCAR. Not ever.

(*They exit.*)

MARIO. I need a drink. Pour me a drink, Rosa.

ROSA. Yes, sir.

MARIO. They'll want the books. Where are they kept?

ROSA. In here. (*She points to the sideboard*)

MARIO. I don't have the key.

(*He takes Oscar's gun from Rosa's hands and shoots the lock off the sideboard*)

ROSA. You work fast.

MARIO. When you're changing the world, speed is your friend.

(*He takes the ledgers and begins to look through them*)

So much money. They stole so much goddamned money! Mafiosos!

ROSA. May God have pity on you, Mario.

MARIO. I've fallen from grace? Branded forever. Isn't that right, Rosa?

ROSA. Yes.

MARIO. In jail...When they're in jail, they'll begin to know what life in this house was like for me.

ROSA. This house is too beautiful to be a jail.

MARIO. When you sleep in a single bed against the wall and on the other side of the wall your mother sleeps, and it's been going on like this for more than fifty years, it is a jail.

ROSA. You should have moved the bed.

MARIO. Get me a brandy.

(**ROSA** *pours a brandy and hands it to* **MARIO.** *The lights fade to black.*)

END OF PLAY

Also by
Eduardo Machado...

Broken Eggs

The Cook

Havana is Waiting

Kissing Fidel

Modern Ladies of Guanabacoa

Once Removed